D0529642

NOW YOU CAN READ....
Little Red Hen

STORY ADAPTED BY LUCY KINCAID

ILLUSTRATED BY BELINDA LYON

BRIMAX BOOKS • CAMBRIDGE • ENGLAND

Little Red Hen lived with her three friends in a house beside a muddy pool. Little Red Hen was always busy and it was she who kept the house neat and tidy.

"Duck spends too much time swimming.
Pig spends too much time wallowing.
Cat spends too much time sleeping,"
she would cluck crossly as she
swept and dusted and cleaned.
"But I like swimming," said Duck.
"I would rather swim on the pond
than do anything else."

"And I like wallowing," said Pig.
"I would rather wallow in the mud than do anything else."

"And I like sleeping," said Cat.
"I would rather sleep in the sun than do anything else."

One day, when
Little Red Hen
was scratching
about in the
garden looking
for worms, she
found some grains
of wheat.
"Who will help
me plant these
grains of wheat?"
she called to
her three friends.

"Not I," quacked Duck. "I am going for a swim."

"Not I," grunted Pig. "I am going for a wallow."

"Not I," miaowed Cat. "I am too sleepy."

"Then I will plant them myself," said Little Red Hen.

And she did.

She planted the grains in a corner of the garden. She watered them and they began to grow. Each day the shoots grew a little taller. The sun shone on the growing wheat and ripened it, and one day, it was ready to cut.

"Who will help me cut the wheat?" called Little Red Hen.

"Not I," quacked Duck. "I am going for a swim."

"Not I," grunted Pig. "I have found a new patch of mud."

"Not I," miaowed Cat. "I am looking for a place to sleep."

"Then I will cut it myself," said Little Red Hen. And she did. She sharpened the blade and cut the stems of wheat. When they were cut she gathered them together and made them into a large bundle with all the plump golden ears at one end. When she was finished she called her friends. "Who will help me thresh the wheat?" she asked.

"Not I," quacked Duck, and dipped her head into the pond.

"Not I," grunted Pig, and rolled over in the mud.

"Not I," miaowed Cat, and curled up on top of the wall.

"Then I will thresh it myself,"
said Little Red Hen.
And she did.
It was very hard work. It made
her puff and it made her feel
tired. But at last all the grains
had fallen from the ears. She
gathered them up and put them into
a basket.
"Who will take the grains of wheat
to the mill to be ground?" she
called.

"Not I," quacked Duck.
"Not I," grunted Pig.
"Not I," miaowed Cat.
"Then I will take
them to the mill
myself," said
Little Red Hen.
And she did.
The mill stood on
top of a hill so
that the wind
could blow the
sails. It was a
long steep climb.
Little Red Hen was
very tired by the
time she got there.

The miller ground the wheat into flour for her and poured it into a strong linen bag. Little Red Hen put the linen bag into the basket and carried it home.

The next morning, when Little Red
Hen, Duck, Pig and Cat, were having
breakfast, Little Red Hen said,
"Who will help me bake a loaf of
bread today?"
"Not I," quacked Duck, and waddled
outside quickly. "I want to swim
on the pond."

"Not I," grunted Pig, gulping his toast. "I want to wallow in the mud."

"Not I," miaowed Cat, with a lazy yawn. "I want to sleep in the sun."

"Then I will bake it myself," said Little Red Hen.

And she did.

She chopped some wood. She lit the fire. She made the flour into dough. She put the dough into a tin. She put the tin into the oven. And then she waited. Soon a delicious smell wafted through the kitchen.

When the bread was cooked Little
Red Hen took it from the oven and
put it on the windowsill to cool.
"Who will help me eat my loaf of
brown crusty bread?" she called.

"I will," quacked Duck.

"I will," grunted Pig.

"I will," miaowed Cat.

"You are all wrong," said Little Red Hen. "I found the grains of wheat. I planted them. I looked after the wheat. I watered it. I cut it. I threshed it. I carried it to the mill. I made it into bread. So I am going to eat it." And she did, EVERY crumb.

All these appear in the pages
of the story. Can you find them?

red hen

duck

cat

pig